ZIGGY'S MAGIC WISH

BY LAURA BELL

© THE MEDICI SOCIETY LTD · 1988 · Printed in England. ISBN 0 85503 150 6

One morning Ziggy went for a walk in a field near his home. It was the day before his birthday and he felt very excited. Suddenly, in the grass before him, something caught his eye. It was a bright golden coin in the middle of a fairy ring. As he walked home he turned it over in his pocket slowly.

I wonder if it is magic he thought.

There was a full moon that night and Ziggy looked out of his window with the coin in his hand. What shall I wish for? he wondered.

Perhaps a pair of boots, then I could be a mountain climber . . . .

Dizzy descents, not me!

Or even a hot air balloon, then I could float high above the countryside . . . .

Beastly beaks. Look out below!

What about a space suit, then I could be a spaceman on the moon . . . .

Cosmic calamities, not for me!

Maybe a sledge, then I could be an arctic explorer . . . .

Shivering icicles, brrrrr!

I could wish for a suit of armour, then I could be a gallant knight . . . .

Not tonight!

Possibly a pair of flippers, then I could be a deep sea diver . . . .

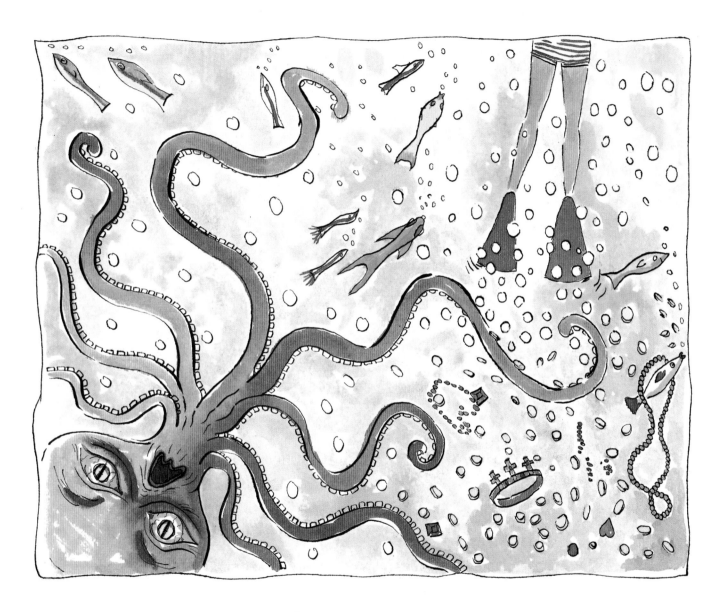

Slimy squids, eeik!

Maybe a telescope, then I could be a Captain on the high seas . . . .

Shiver me timbers, not likely!

What about a box of tricks, then I could be a great magician . . . .

Bouncing bunnies, help!!

Or even a butterfly net, then I could be a jungle explorer . . . .

Blundering buffaloes, no way!

Perhaps I'll just wish for a HUGE BIRTHDAY CAKE
and a party for all my friends.

HAPPY BIRTHDAY ZIGGY — GOODNIGHT !